# A NOTE TO PARENTS

When your children are ready to "step into reading," giving them the right books—and lots of them—is as crucial as giving them the right food to eat. **Step into Reading Books** present exciting stories or information reinforced with lively, colorful illustrations that make learning to read fun, satisfying, and worthwhile. They are priced so that acquiring an entire library of them is affordable. And they are beginning readers with an important difference—they're written on three levels.

**Step 1 Books,** with their very large type and extremely simple vocabulary, have been created for the very youngest readers. **Step 2 Books** are both longer and slightly more difficult. **Step 3 Books,** written to mid-second-grade reading levels, are for the child who has acquired even greater reading skills.

To Patti and Chris Kirigan
—J.C.

For Dan—L.M.

*Library of Congress Cataloging-in-Publication Data:* Cole, Joanna. Norma Jean, jumping bean. (Step into reading. A Step 2 book) SUMMARY: Norma Jean, whose love of jumping might be a bit excessive, stops her favorite activity after her friends complain, but participation in the school Olympics proves there is a time and place for jumping. [1. Jumping—Fiction] I. Munsinger, Lynn, ill. II. Title. III. Series: Step into reading. Step 2 book. PZ7.C67346No 1987 [E] 86-15588 ISBN: 0-394-88668-2 (trade); 0-394-98668-7 (lib. bdg.)

Manufactured in the United States of America 2 3 4 5 6 7 8 9 0

STEP INTO READING is a trademark of Random House, Inc.

Step into Reading

# Norma Jean, Jumping Bean

By Joanna Cole

Illustrated by Lynn Munsinger

A Step 2 Book

Random House 🏠 New York

Norma Jean liked to jump.

In the morning
she jumped out of bed.

She jumped

into her clothes.

She jumped

down the stairs.

Norma Jean jumped
all the way to school.
She jumped past
Amy, Sam,
Nell, and Ted.
"Wow!" said Ted.
"Look at her go!
That Norma Jean
never stops jumping!"

"Hello hello hello!"

she called to her friends.

That morning

Miss Jones read a book

to the class.

It was a very good book.

But Norma Jean did not

sit still long enough

to hear the story.

At playtime

Norma Jean and Nell

built a tower of blocks.

Norma Jean was so excited.

She jumped up and down.

Oh, no!

No more tower.

At lunch

Sam gave Norma Jean

a cupcake.

Norma Jean was so happy.

She jumped up and down.

Oh, no!

Her milk spilled

all over Sam.

"Norma Jean,

please sit still,"

said Miss Jones.

"This is not the time

or place for jumping."

After school

Norma Jean went

to visit Ted.

"Hello hello hello!"

she shouted to Ted.

"Will you play with me?"

"Okay," said Ted.

"Let's get on my seesaw."

But Norma Jean bounced too hard.

Ted almost flew off the seesaw.

"I don't want to play anymore,"
Ted said.

"I wonder why Ted
is mad at me,"
said Norma Jean.

Then she jumped over to Amy's house.

Amy was playing in her pool.

"Hello hello hello!"

said Norma Jean.

"May I play too?"

Amy said, "Sure.

Jump in!"

That was the wrong thing
to say to Norma Jean!
SPLASH!

Amy got out of the pool.

"Why did you get out?"

asked Norma Jean.

"We are having so much fun!"

Amy said,

"<u>You</u> are having fun.

<u>I</u> am going inside.

It is no fun playing

with a jumping bean!"

Now Norma Jean knew why
her friends were mad at her.

The next day
Norma Jean walked
to school very slowly.

There was a big puddle.

All the other kids

jumped over it.

But Norma Jean did not jump.

Norma Jean said,

"I don't want to be a jumping bean.

No more jumping for Norma Jean."

So she walked

through the puddle

and got her feet all wet.

In the school yard

kids were running around

and playing catch

and jumping rope.

"There's Norma Jean,"
said Amy.
"Come jump with us."
But Norma Jean
said no.

Norma Jean said,

"I don't want to be a jumping bean.

No more jumping for Norma Jean."

And she just stood there

and watched the other kids jump rope.

At the end of the day

Miss Jones told the class

that Field Day was coming soon.

There were going to be

lots of races.

Ted wanted to be

in the egg-and-spoon race.

Amy and Sam

said they would be

in the wheelbarrow race.

Nell asked if she could be

in the rope-climbing contest.

FIELD DAY
EGG + SPOON RACE
TED
WHEELBARROW RACE
SAM + AMY
ROPE CLIMBING
NELL
JUMPING CONTESTS

"Now, who will be in

the jumping contests?"

asked Miss Jones.

Everybody shouted,

"Norma Jean! Norma Jean!

She is the best jumper in school!"

But Norma Jean said,

"I don't want to be a jumping bean.

No more jumping for Norma Jean."

Ted said,

"I miss the old Norma Jean.

She was fun,

even if she did jump a lot."

On Field Day,

Ted won

the egg-and-spoon race.

Norma Jean was very happy.

She yelled,

"Hooray! Hooray!"

Amy and Sam

came in first

in the wheelbarrow race.

Norma Jean yelled,

"Hooray hooray hooray!"

And she jumped up and down

just a little bit.

Nell won

the rope-climbing contest.

Norma Jean was so excited,
she jumped out
on the field.

Norma Jean was
just in time for
the hurdles,

the high jump,

and the potato-sack race.

She won them all.

"Hooray hooray hooray!"

shouted the kids in Miss Jones's class.

Norma Jean was very happy.

But she did not jump up and down.

She stood very still.

Miss Jones pinned

a blue ribbon

on Norma Jean.

It said,

"Norma Jean, Champion Jumping Bean."

What did Norma Jean do then?

Norma Jean jumped for joy.

She jumped

and she jumped

and she jumped

all the way home.

After all,

there <u>is</u> a time

and a place

for jumping.